Serge Prengel

Bedtime Stories For Your Inner Child™

Active Pause®

Published by Active Pause®, New York, NY.

ISBN: 978-1-892482-32-7

Contents

These stories are meant to be read
With your voice, not just your eyes.

Please read them out loud to others
Or speak them softly to yourself.

The Cat & The Box

A Fable About Feeling Stuck

Once upon a
time,
there was a cat
who was
stuck in
a box.

How did she get there?
It doesn't matter.

We all get stuck at some point
or another,

in a box,
in a career,
in a role,
or in a story we
tell ourselves
about who we
are.

The box had once felt safe. Now it felt confining.

She so wanted to get
out of that box!

The more frustrated she got, the more she thought:
"I could do it if only I had this or that."
We all feel life would be so much easier "if only we had this or that," don't we?

Of course, this kind of thinking didn't work any better
for her than it does for you and me.
She stayed stuck inside the box.

In her
frustration,
she kept
telling
herself:

*"I could do
it if only I
<u>was</u> this or
that."*

Life would
be so much
easier "if
only we
were this or
that,"
wouldn't
it?

Did it work? Nah. She was even more stuck.

So what was it that finally
enabled her to
get out of
the box?

She remembered that feeling stuck
usually comes from avoiding
difficult feelings.

Our mind tenses up, so to speak, to avoid them.

This tension inside *feels like* we are trapped in a box...
in a prison...
in a straightjacket...

But, in reality, it's something inside us that's trapped.

So she asked: *"What is it that's trapped inside?"*

Gently, she allowed herself to feel
what was stuck inside...

Was it anger?..
Sadness?..
Fear?..

It was fear indeed.

She felt cowed by a ferocious internal voice.

A voice demanding
that she *should* be this...
that she *should* do that...

As she became aware
of the critical voice,

she was able to
see
its demands for
what
they really were:

Unrealistic
demands.

And she was now able to walk away from the box.

Scissorship

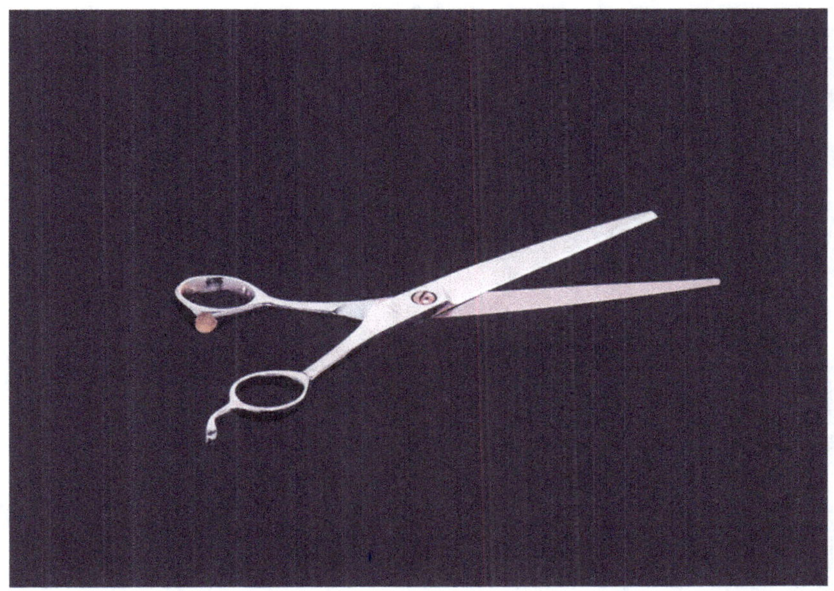

A Whimsical Fable About Empowerment

Let us now enter the world of the Fable...

It is a world where the strangest creatures
roam and interact.

So we won't be too surprised that
our hero and narrator is neither a person
nor an animal...

I was born among
Scissors

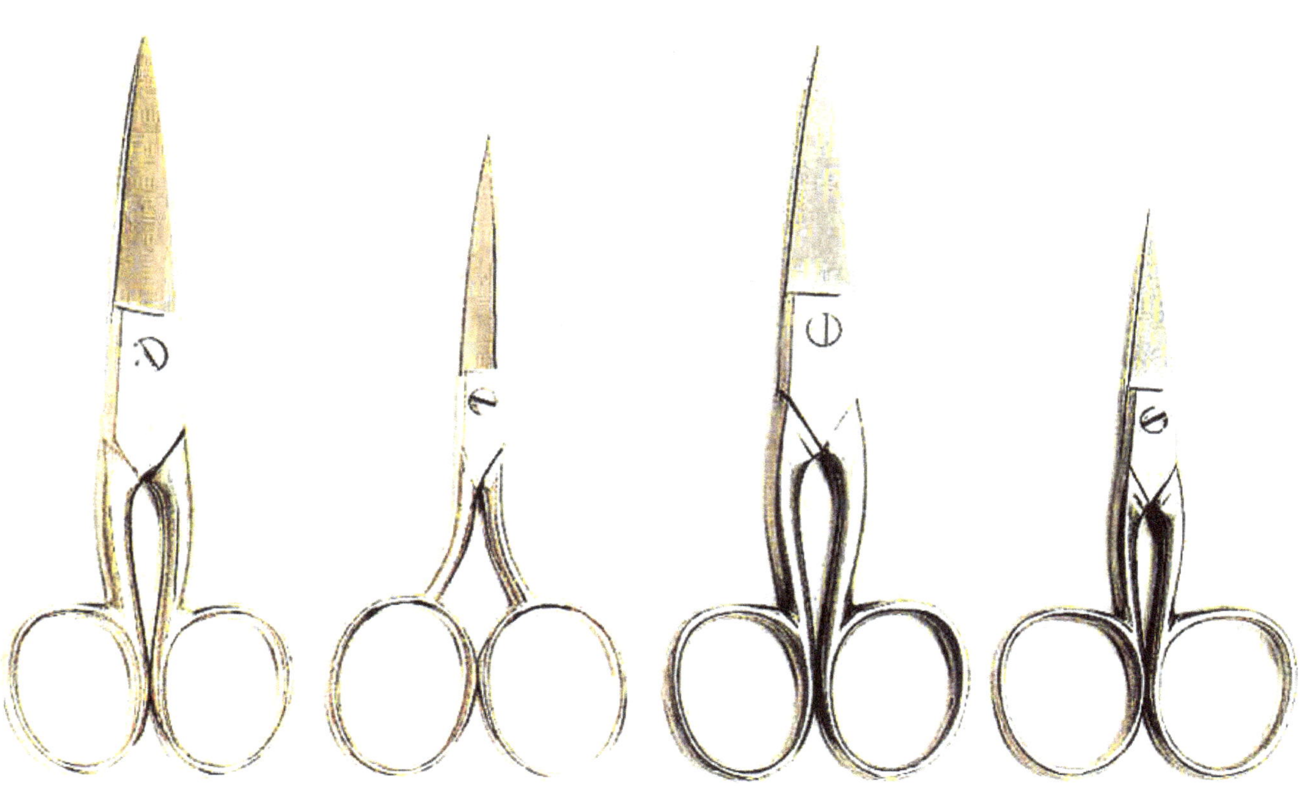

From childhood on,
I was taught to
take pride in
how sharp
we scissors are.

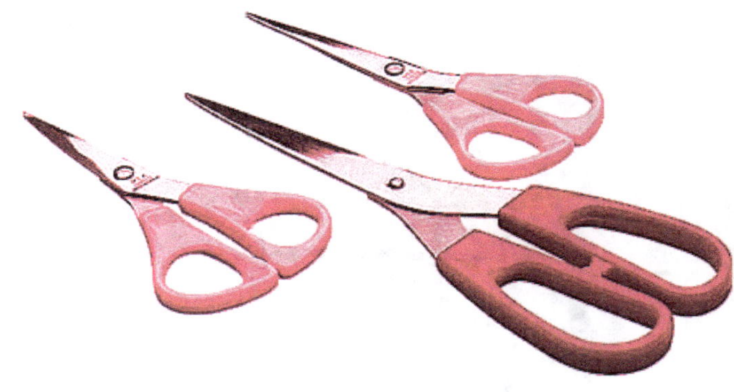

However, I soon came to notice that the tone was quite different when the adults thought we kids weren't listening.

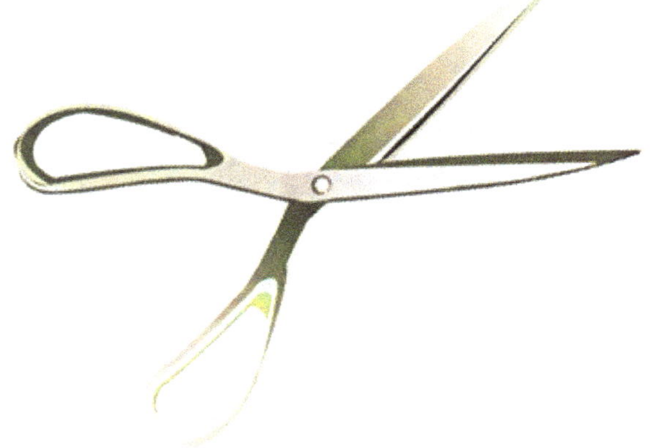

All this pride of Scissorship
was just a charade to impress
kids with

a false sense of strength
and security.

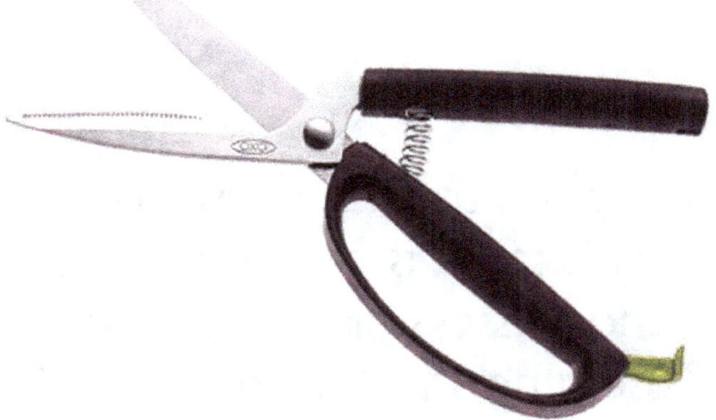

The sad truth is : Scissors live in fear of Rocks!
All it takes is one encounter with a Rock...
and Scissors are blunted out of any
usefulness... dishonored... discarded...

As for me:

I came to understand
what other scissors
were going through.

And I resolved
that it wouldn't
happen to me.

I wasn't going to spend the
rest of my life living in fear.

It took a grueling regimen of exercise,
tons of nutritional supplements,
and an iron will...

I worked hard at
getting the rough
edges I so lacked.
Not only did I look
like a true-born
Rock...

I came to think like
a Rock and feel
like a Rock.

Native Rocks now saw me as one of them.

Oh! Horror!

This is when
I discovered that,
far from savoring
their power,
Rocks actually
live in terror of
the looming threat
of that most
lethal of enemies:

Paper.

Paper is so much less substantial than Rock, but it has devious ways to use that very flaw to its own advantage. Paper wraps itself around things, yes, even around mighty Rock.

I was crushed,
but not for long.

Yoga...
Pilates...
Drastic dieting...
Visualizations...
Meditations...
I did it all...

It was excruciating.
But well worth it:
I was on my way
to becoming Paper.

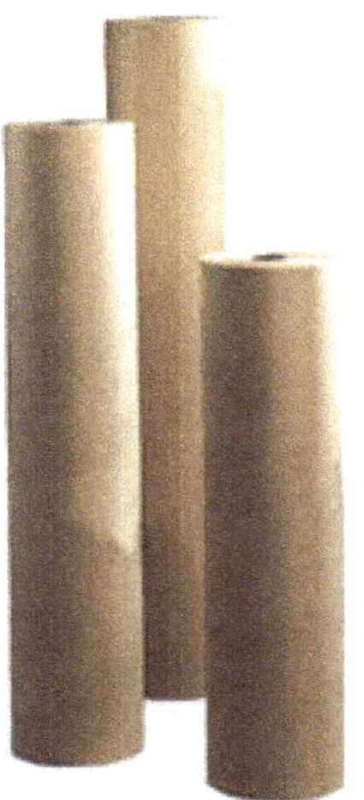

At long last, I was
able to mix in freely
with my fellow
Papers.

I felt giddy with

exhilaration…
until
I heard
what they
were talking about:

Papers live in terror
of Scissors!

At long last, it dawned on me:

It really has not worked
for me to bemoan
my shortcomings
and try to be
what I'm not.

So now,
instead of dwelling
on what I don't have,
I choose to focus on what
I have.

And so it came to be that I regained my sense of
Scissorship.

In the moment

A fable about living in the moment

It was a beautiful Sunday in the park.

People were
gathered
around
the
storyteller.

Tell us,
O
Storyteller,
How can we
unleash the
power of
Now?

He said:

We yearn to live in
the present

But the present is hard
to grasp

Caught as it is
between the past and
the future.

Oooh, they said. Please, Storyteller, Tell us more.

So he pointed
to a game
that was going on:

A young man
holding a bat
Waiting to strike a
ball.

This ball is
not
suspended
in mid-air,
he said.

What keeps it in the air right
now is the momentum it got
when the pitcher threw it.

As for the
bat:
It's not
suspended
in mid-air,
either.

A moment ago, the man raised the bat
Preparing for a future when it would hit
the ball.

The present
moment
is but a bridge
between the
past
and the
future.

Ahhh,
said the listeners.
And how do we
walk on this
bridge?

Indeed,
said the
storyteller.
How do we?

We slow down.
We look. We try to see what truly is.

During the
moment,
there is
no beginning,
no end,
and no next
moment.

In that one fleeting moment
lies immortality.

Which, of course,
disappears the next moment.

Aha,
said the
listeners.
And they
started
singing:

Row, row, row the boat. Gently down the stream

It was
a beautiful
Sunday
in late
Summer.

The moment
is long past
But the sense
of it
is very
present.

About

Serge Prengel

Serge Prengel is in private practice in New York and a co-founder of the *Integrative Focusing Therapy* online training program. He has been exploring creative approaches to mindfulness: how to live with an embodied sense of meaning and purpose. He is the author of *15-Minute Self-Motivation Workbook* and *Ayshu*.

Active Pause®

http://activepause.com